FREDERICK FERDINAND FOX

FREDERICK FERDINAND FOX

written and illustrated by

EDWARD MILLER

Crown Publishers, Inc.   New York

Published by Crown Publishers, Inc., 225 Park Avenue South, New York, New York 10003
and represented in Canada by the Canadian MANDA Group
CROWN is a trademark of Crown Publishers, Inc.
Manufactured in Japan.
Library of Congress Cataloging-in-Publication Data
Miller, Edward (Edward Ward). Frederick Ferdinand Fox. Summary: A fox relates the wartime
events in which he conducted himself heroically and became postmaster general for the kingdom
of Coralville. [1. Foxes—Fiction. 2. War—Fiction] I. Title.
PZ7.M61286Fr 1986 [E] 86-8847
ISBN 0-517-56356-8
10 9 8 7 6 5 4 3 2 1
First Edition

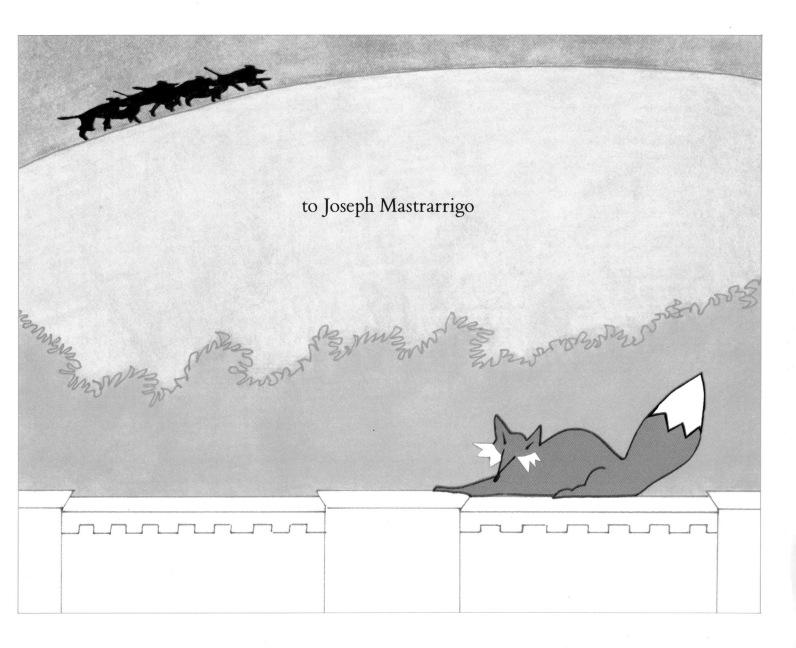

to Joseph Mastrarrigo

My name is Frederick Ferdinand Fox. For generations my family have been mail carriers for the Kingdom of Coralville. But there has never been one as famous as I. This is the story to tell you why.

Ten years ago the Emperor Benedict of Weedlock came sweeping across the countryside, conquering every town as he went by. After taking possession of the land around us, he declared war on Coralville.

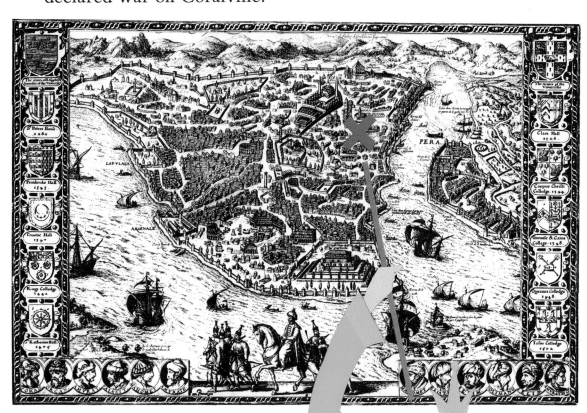

The king called an urgent meeting of all his councilmen. I was delivering mail to the palace at the time. As I walked past the conference room, a councilman yelled out, "Stop, Frederick!" To my surprise he was talking to me. I went inside.

The councilman turned and said to the king, "It is most important that our secret messages reach the commander on the battlefield without them getting into the hands of the enemy. I elect Frederick for the job."

I was then appointed by His Majesty to deliver the secret messages.

There was no time to waste. The king gave me the first set of plans and said, "Beware, Frederick! Emperor Benedict has secret agents who would do anything to stop you." I bowed farewell to the king and was on my way.

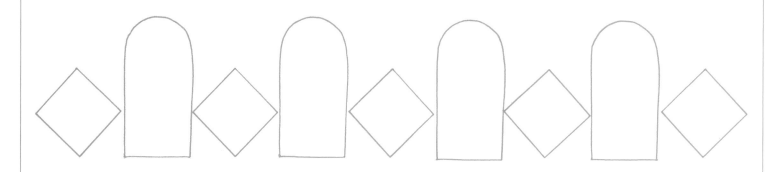

I could sense danger as I left the palace, but I was not afraid. I knew the secret agents would not suspect a mailman as a messenger.

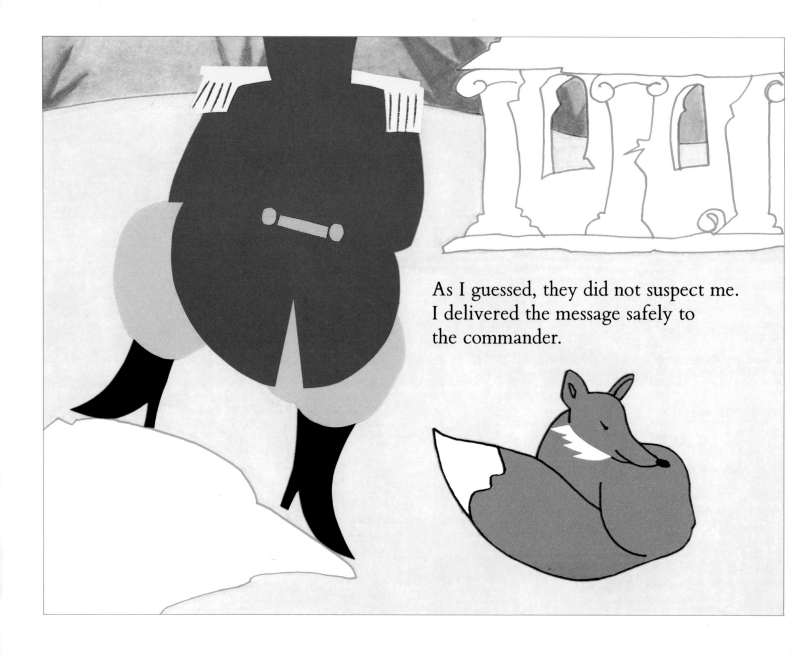

As I guessed, they did not suspect me.
I delivered the message safely to
the commander.

The next morning the king summoned me to the palace to deliver another message. This time my job would be more dangerous. I knew the agents could not be outwitted a second time.

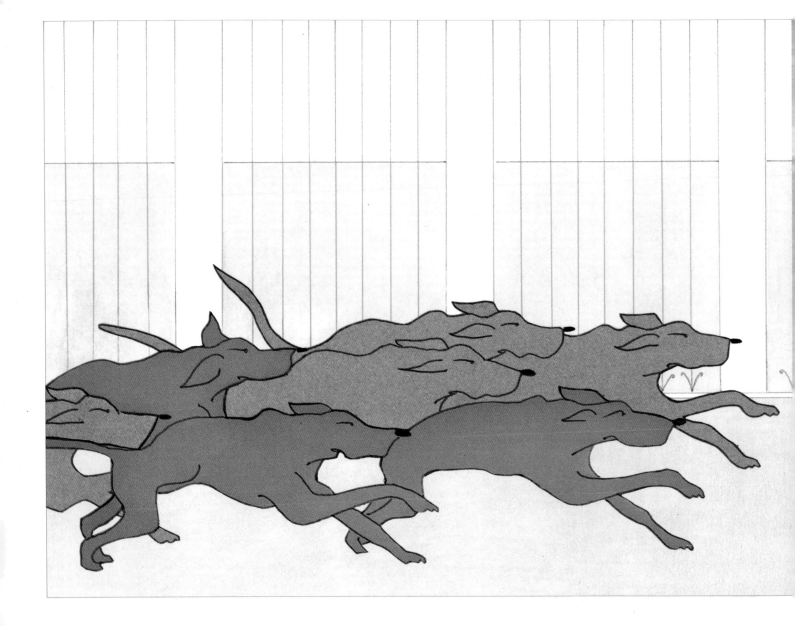

I no sooner got out the palace gates when ten secret
agents spotted me with the sealed royal message.
I ran for my life.

I managed to escape and deliver the written orders to the commander.

The next morning I was summoned again to the palace. The king told me it was most important that these instructions were delivered because they were the plans to win the war. I bowed farewell and was on my way.

I no sooner got out the front door when twenty secret agents came chasing me. I ran for my life. They chased me for hours. I could not seem to get away.

Fortunately, I saw an open store door and ran inside.

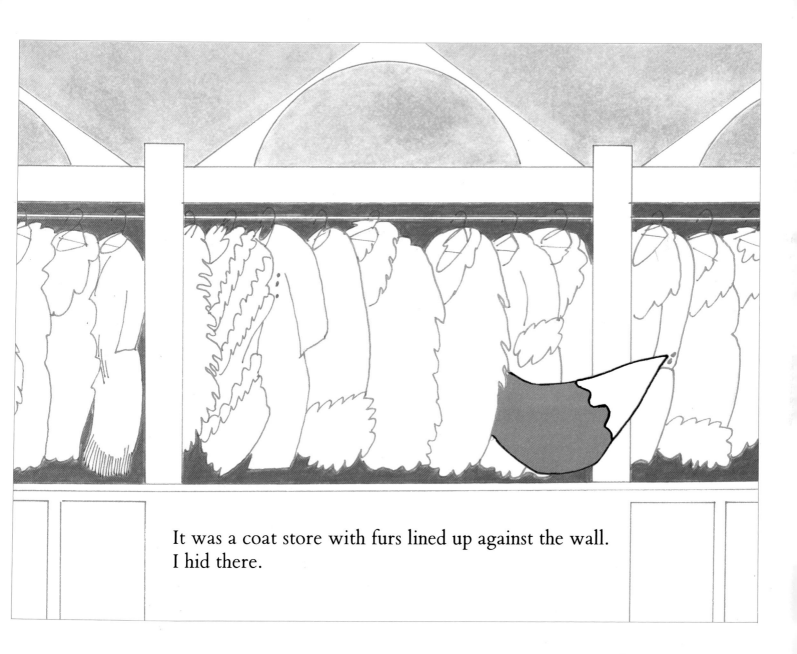

It was a coat store with furs lined up against the wall.
I hid there.

One of the dogs spotted me going in and followed.

The dog was getting closer and closer. I did not dare move an inch.

All of a sudden a shopper picked me up, mistaking me for a red fox stole, and tried me on. "A perfect fit!" she exclaimed and took me home.

I was now traveling safely on the shoulders of a
shopper. A perfect disguise!

To the shopper's surprise I leaped off when we got to the edge of town. I ran to the battlefield and delivered the plans safely to the commander. The commander read them and said, "With these plans victory will be ours. You will be a hero, Frederick!"

The war is over now, and of course Emperor Benedict was defeated.
Peace now resides throughout the countryside once again.

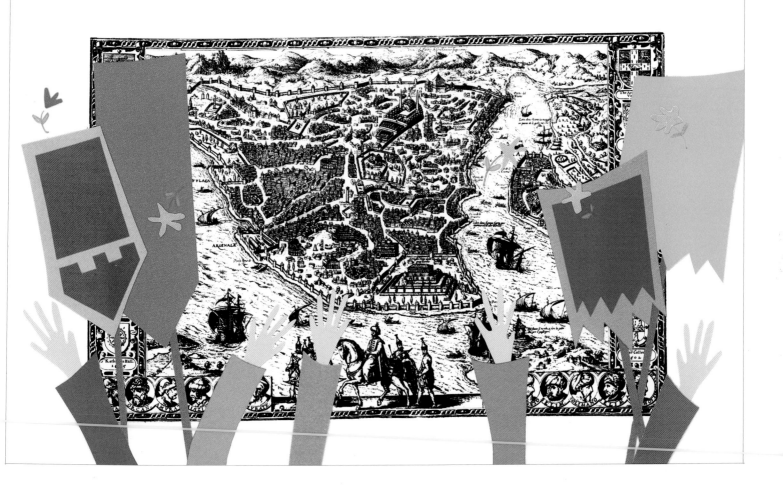

As for me, at the victory parade
I was appointed Postmaster General.

Every year on the anniversary of our victory, the commander
and the king send me a royal message that says, "Long live
Frederick Ferdinand Fox!"

The End